LISTEN, LISTEN!

by Ylla

Story by Crosby Newell Bonsall

Planned by CHARLES RADO
Designed by LUC BOUCHAGE

HARPER & BROTHERS   *Publishers*   New York

Once there were two little cats.

One little cat named Purr.

One little cat named Mew.

One little cat named Purr slept all the time

except when he was listening.

One little cat named Mew talked all the time

except when he was dreaming.

He was dreaming now.

"Stop dreaming," said Purr and yanked Mew's whisker.

"Stop dreaming and talk to me because

I'm awake. But not for long."

"Well," said Mew, watching his dream slip away,

"if you'll stay awake I'll tell you a story.

I'll tell you a story about a dog who didn't

and a cat who did."

"Did what?" said Purr.

"Just listen," said Mew.

"Once there was a dog,"
said Mew,
"who never,
never,
no, never
ever

COMBED HIS HAIR!"

"Never?" said Purr.
"Never," said Mew.

"He was a shaggy dog," said Mew, "with a round, shiny nose. His hair grew and grew like the grass in the spring until he couldn't see where he was going. So he sat down.

"He didn't see the black cat looking at him. But he knew it was a cat because his round, shiny nose told him so. 'Why don't you comb your hair?' said the cat.

" 'My hair grows and grows like the grass in the spring,' said the shaggy dog, 'and whoever heard of combing the grass?'

" 'Nonsense,' said the cat, 'you can't see anything. You can't see a ball bouncing over a wall. You can't see a stick to pick up. I'll comb your hair for you. I'll comb it with my paw and it won't hurt a bit. Hold still,' said the cat, 'be quiet,' said the cat, 'DON'T WIGGLE,' said the cat.

"So the black cat combed the shaggy dog's hair. She patted his bangs, and poked at his whiskers, and soon she uncovered his two bright eyes. 'Now,' said the cat, 'that's better.'

"And she patted the nose of the shaggy dog who wasn't so shaggy now.

" 'Run along,' said the cat, 'there's a ball and a stick and a bowl of stew waiting for you.' And the shaggy dog ran away to look."

"Did he find the stew?" asked Purr.

"He did," said Mew, "and now I'll tell you a story about a dog who wished for a chin tickler.

"Everything prickled and nothing tickled his chin as he wanted it tickled. At last," Mew said, "he saw a cat. 'Will you tickle my chin, little cat?' the dog cried. 'Will you tickle my chin—not prickle my chin—and tickle and tickle some more?'

" 'I never prickle,' the cat said, 'I tickle.'

"Now the little dog sits with the tickly cat tucked under his tickled chin as tickled as tickled can be. And there's never a prickle in all the tickles that tickle his tickly chin."

Mew waited for Purr to say something.

All he heard was a drowsy sound.

"Wake up, Purr, wake up and listen," Mew cried.

"Listen! I haven't told you about the cats
who looked."

"Mmmmmmmmmmmm?" said Purr.

"You promised," said Mew, "you promised
if I stopped dreaming
and told you stories
you'd stay awake."

"Mmmmmmmmm," said Purr.

"Open your eyes," said Mew.

He patted Purr's head with his paw.

"Open your eyes."

"Tell me about the cats who looked," said Purr
in a sleepy voice. "I'm awake,
but . . . not . . . for . . . long."

"Once upon a time," said Mew,
"there were two cats who were
always looking."
"What for?" said Purr.
"Anything," said Mew, "they
looked for anything at all.
That way they almost always
found something.

"They looked up,
they looked down,
one way
and another,

"and sometimes
they looked
and found
only each other.

"But one day," said Mew, "they did find something. They looked up and found a ball of string and they pulled it.

They pulled,
and pulled,
and pulled,
and PULLED
that
ball
of
string.
And
all
at once
that

ball of string wasn't there any more. Sometimes there is a kite on the end of a ball of string, or a sailboat, or a brown cow. But there wasn't anything on the end, not even another ball of string. It happens you know, especially if you pull."

"But if you don't pull you won't find out," said Purr.

"That's it, exactly," said Mew.

"After that," Mew went on,

"those cats sat in a tree

and looked.

For looking was what they did best."

"Did they see the ball of string?" asked Purr.

Mew said, "I have already

explained about the

ball of string.

You're not listening."

"I'm sleepy," said Purr.

"Wake up," said Mew, "because

those cats saw something else.

They saw a lonely kitten

and I'll tell you the story.

" 'Puppy, please
talk to me,'
said the kitten.
'This sky is
so big and
so wide that
I'm lonely.'
" 'Excuse me,' said
the puppy, 'I
was looking at a
rabbit asleep
in the grass.

" 'But I won't
chase that
rabbit. I'll
stay here be-
side you and
be your friend.'
" 'I feel better
now,' said the
kitten, 'it's
nice to have
a friend.'

" 'Why, there are friends all around you,' the puppy said, 'but you'll never find them until you lift your head and open your eyes. Go look and you'll see.'

"So the kitten started out. She met a turtle. And it's a very nice thing to talk to turtles," said Mew.

" 'I'd ask you in,' said the turtle, 'but my house is only big enough for me.'

" 'Aren't you lonely in your little house?' asked the kitten.

" 'Oh no,' said the turtle, 'I have many friends. Of course, I do spend a lot of time in the house, but then I can go home whenever I like, and I never, never get lost.'

" 'That's true,' said the kitten, 'but you can't roll in clover, and chase your tail.'

" 'That's for kittens,' said the turtle, 'and even if we can't do the same things we can be friends.' And they were," said Mew. "That's how there came to be a kitten and a turtle on a log in the sun."

"A kittle and a turten," said Purr sleepily.

"Silly," said Mew, "sit up and I'll tell you another story.

"Once there was a little cat who lived in a suitcase with a dog. She thought she was a dog, too. If he barked, she tried to bark. The dog would say, 'You silly thing, don't you know you're a cat?' But the little cat didn't believe him and they sat in the suitcase and sulked.

"Once the little cat did a terrible thing," said Mew. "SHE CHASED A CAT! 'See here,' said the dog, 'that's for dogs to do. When there are cats to be chased I will chase them. You must learn that you are not a dog. Just look at me and you will see we don't look at all alike. I am a great big, tall, strong dog. You are a foolish little cat. You will never be as tall as I.' He stood up on his back legs. The little cat watched carefully. 'Fiddle-dee-dee,' she said and—

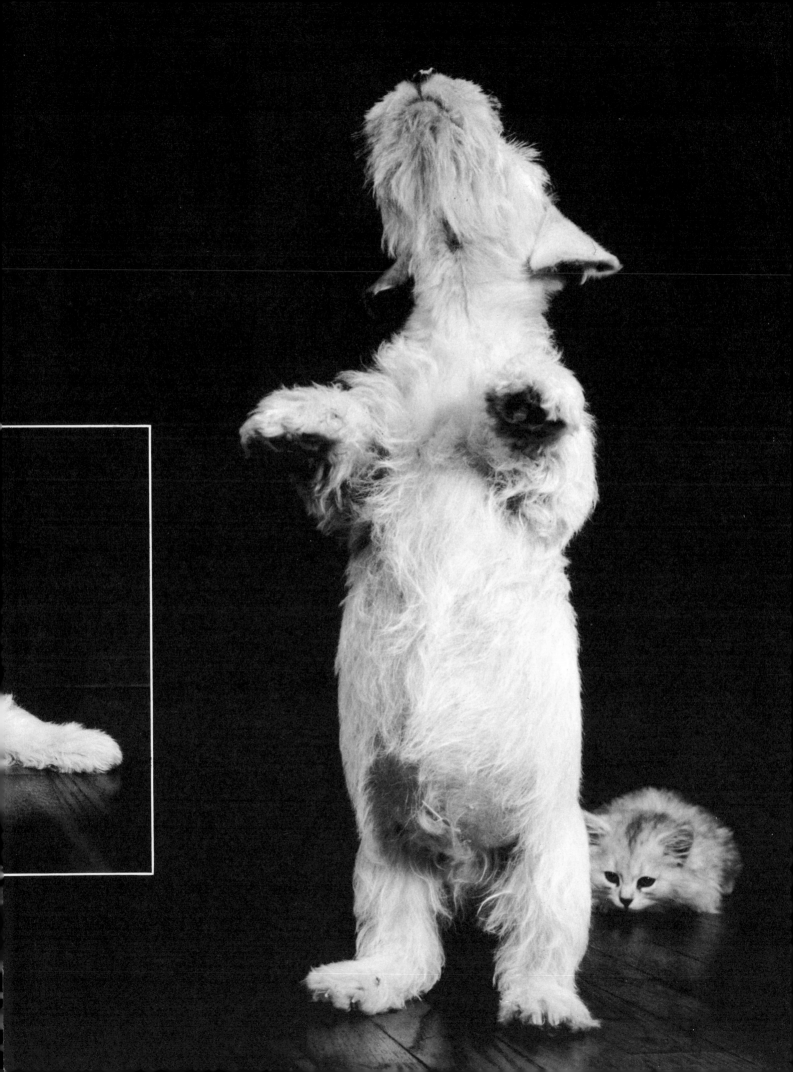

"The little cat stood up

on

her

two

back

legs

as tall, as tall

as that great big dog.

"The dog and the cat still live in the suitcase,

and the cat still thinks she's a dog.

I know," said Mew,

"because she chased ME once.

Did you ever hear of such a thing?"

Mew listened.

"Hey, Purr," he cried,

"are you asleep?"

Purr was.

"Aw, shucks," said Mew.

"Ho-hum," said Mew.

And two little cats lay fast asleep.